Curly Crow

Goes Camping:
Surviving in the Wilderness

Written by:
Nicholas Aragon

ISBN: 978-1-957701-01-1 (Hardback)
ISBN: 978-1-957701-03-5 (Paperback)
ISBN: 978-1-957701-02-8 (Ebook)

Library of Congress Control Number: 2022935450

Printed by Curly Crow in the United States of America.

First edition 2022.

support@curlycrow.com
Albuquerque, New Mexico

www.CurlyCrow.com

I dedicate the Curly Crow Children's Book Series to
my two beautiful daughters (Merriah and Mahli) and
my amazing wife Amanda. And, to Gramma Barb who
started it all. My mission is to inspire others and help
heal the human spirit through art.

Nicholas Aragon

Curly Crow is a curious little bird who lives with her family next to a café in New Mexico. Other than eating from the café's dumpster, which contains some of the best thrown-away food in the city, her favorite pastime is exploring the world.

One day, Curly's dad says, "Let's do something exciting!" "Sure! But what can we do? There are so many choices," says Curly. They decide that, whatever they do, it will definitely be an adventure.

Curly and Dad begin to brainstorm ideas. Dad suggests trying out a new dumpster. "Maybe it will have some tasty food that we've never tried." But Curly is not convinced. "Let's go out into nature," she suggests.

"That's it!" Dad exclaims. "Pack your bags. Let's go camping!" Curly can't believe it. She has never gone camping, and it sounds like so much fun.

Curly packs her supplies: a board game, a flashlight, and some bug spray. She will obviously need all these items in the wild. Her father packs a tent, warm clothes, a walking stick, a compass, and food.

Curly and her dad fly off in search of adventure. The sights they see as they look down from up above are beautiful. But unfortunately, somewhere along the way their food falls out of their packs!

Curly looks around and doesn't see any dumpsters anywhere. "What will we eat?" she asks. "We will have to live off the land," Dad says.